CAVEBOY
IS BORED!

Agnes and Clarabelle

Agnes and Clarabelle Celebrate!

Stinky Spike the Pirate Dog

Stinky Spike and the Royal Rescue

Wallace and Grace Take the Case

Wallace and Grace and the Cupcake Caper

Wallace and Grace and the Lost Puppy

The Adventures of Caveboy

Caveboy Is Bored!

Caveboy Is a Hit!

CAVEBOY IS BORED!

SUDIPTA BARDHAN-QUALLEN
ILLUSTRATED BY ERIC WIGHT

BLOOMSBURY
CHILDREN'S BOOKS
NEW YORK LONDON OXFORD NEW DELHI SYDNEY

To J., the ooga to my booga —S. B.-Q.

To Isla, Finn, Killian, Abbie, and Ethan
—E. W.

BLOOMSBURY CHILDREN'S BOOKS
Bloomsbury Publishing Inc., part of Bloomsbury Publishing Plc
1385 Broadway, New York, NY 10018

BLOOMSBURY, BLOOMSBURY CHILDREN'S BOOKS, and the Diana logo are trademarks of
Bloomsbury Publishing Plc

First published in the United States of America in August 2017 by Bloomsbury Children's Books
Paperback edition published in February 2019

ISBN 978-1-68119-046-4 (paperback)

The Library of Congress has cataloged the hardcover edition as follows:
Names: Bardhan-Quallen, Sudipta, author. | Wight, Eric, illustrator.
Title: Caveboy Is bored! / by Sudipta Bardhan-Quallen ; illustrated by Eric Wight.
Description: New York : Bloomsbury, August 2017. | Series: Read & bloom |
Summary: Most days Caveboy has a lot to do, but because today Mama is busy hunting and Papa is
repainting their cave, he is so bored he might even play with Sister.
Identifiers: LCCN 2016037693 (print) | LCCN 2016045103 (e-book)
ISBN 978-1-68119-045-7 (hardcover)
ISBN 978-1-68119-127-0 (e-book) • ISBN 978-1-68119-128-7 (e-PDF)
Subjects: | CYAC: Prehistoric peoples—Fiction. | Boredom—Fiction. | Play—Fiction. | Humorous stories. |
BISAC: JUVENILE FICTION / Readers / Chapter Books. | JUVENILE FICTION / Humorous Stories. |
JUVENILE FICTION / Social Issues / Friendship.
Classification: LCC PZ7.B25007 Cav 2017 (print) | LCC PZ7.B25007 (e-book) | DDC [E]—dc23
LC record available at https://lccn.loc.gov/2016037693

Art created with Photoshop
Typeset in Chaparral Pro and Tiki Island • Book design by John Candell
Printed in China by C&C Offset Printing Co., Ltd., Shenzhen, Guangdong
1 3 5 7 9 10 8 6 4 2

All papers used by Bloomsbury Publishing Plc are natural, recyclable products
made from wood grown in well-managed forests. The manufacturing processes
conform to the environmental regulations of the country of origin.

TABLE OF CONTENTS

CHAPTER 1
Caveboy Wants to Play

Caveboy's days are filled with lots of cool things.

He takes care of his pet rock. He practices his baseskull skills. He races with his friend Mags. He thumps things with his club.

Most days, Caveboy is very busy and very happy.

But today, Caveboy is not happy. He has already fed his pet rock and taken him for a walk. He has already practiced baseskull with Papa *and* Mama. He has already thumped a bush, a rock, and a giant puddle. He does not have anything left to do today. So Caveboy is bored.

"You should go play," Mama says. "It is a beautiful day."

Caveboy thinks that is a very good idea. He wants to play. But he has a problem. Mama is busy hunting. Papa is busy repainting their cave. Mags is busy with her bone flute lesson.

"There is no one to play with," Caveboy whines.

Then someone says, "I can play!"

The voice is coming from someone small. Small, but loud.

"Is that you, Mags?" Caveboy asks. "Are you done with your lesson?"

"No!" the voice yells. "I am not Mags. But I can play!"

Now Caveboy can hear that this voice does not sound like Mags. This voice is high and screechy. Caveboy covers his ears.

"I can play!" the voice shouts one

last time. Caveboy knows the voice is close. It sounds like it is coming from the other side of Caveboy's cave.

Then Sister peeks out from behind the rock. "Play with me, Caveboy!" she cries.

Caveboy crosses his arms. He stomps one foot. He says, "I am not playing with you, Sister! You are too small. You cannot run fast. You are

afraid of everything. And, worst of all, sisters always smell like burps."

Sister scrunches her eyebrows together. "We do not!" she snaps.

But Caveboy does not listen. He leaves.

He walks through the woods toward the Big Stump. *Who can I play with?* Caveboy wonders.

Then he sees a rock. It looks like his pet rock. But it is bigger and cooler. So Caveboy yells, "Now I can play!"

Caveboy runs to the rock. He says, "I say OOGA, you say BOOGA."

But the rock does not talk. And that is no fun.

“This is boring,” mumbles Caveboy. “I will play with someone else.”

Someone taps Caveboy on the shoulder. When he turns around, he sees it is Sister. “Play with me!” she shouts.

But Caveboy does not listen. “No,” he snaps, “I will not.”

“Then who will you play with?” Sister asks.

Caveboy looks around. He sees a

tree. He yells, “I will play with the tree!”

He runs to the tree. He says, “I say OOGA, you say BOOGA.”

But the tree does not talk. And that is no fun.

"This is boring," grumbles Caveboy. "I will play with someone else."

Someone tugs on Caveboy's arm. When he looks, he sees it is Sister again. She hollers, "Play with me!"

But Caveboy does not listen.

Caveboy sees a saber-tooth tiger.

He yells, "Play!"

He runs to the saber-tooth tiger.

He says, "I say OOGA, you say BOOGA."

"OOGA!"

The saber-tooth tiger says,

ROAR!

And that is no fun at all!

"Ahhhhhhh!" screams Caveboy. He runs and runs.

When he stops, he pants, "Saber-tooth tiger is too hungry! I will play with someone else."

He looks around. There is no one left. "Rock cannot play with me. Tree cannot play with me. Saber-tooth tiger wants to eat me."

Caveboy sighs. "Now what will I do?"

Caveboy is not happy.

And Caveboy is still bored.

Then someone squeals, "I will play!"

The voice is high and screechy. Caveboy looks around.

"I will play!" she yells.

The voice is coming from someone small. Small, but not *too* small.

"I will play!" she squeals one last time.

Caveboy scratches his head. He taps one foot. He says, "But sisters smell like burps."

Caveboy looks at Sister. He takes a deep breath. Then, in his loudest, fiercest voice, he yells,

In Sister's loudest, fiercest voice, she replies,

What? Caveboy does not know what to say. He steps closer to Sister.

"OOGA?" he says again.

"BOOGA!" she says again.

Maybe Sister can *play,* Caveboy thinks. He grabs her hand. "Come with me!" he shouts.

They run to the rock. "OOGA!" says Caveboy.

"BOOGA!" Sister replies. Then

she shows Caveboy some games to play with the rock. She shows him a hopping game and a drawing game.

"That was fun," says Caveboy. "Thank you, Sister."

"We are not done!" Sister shouts. She points to the tree.

They run to it. "OOGA!" says Caveboy.

"BOOGA!" says Sister. Then she shows Caveboy a climbing game and a chasing game.

"That was even more fun," says Caveboy. "Thank you, Sister."

"We are still not done!" Sister shouts. She points to the saber-tooth tiger.

They run to him. "OOGA!" says Caveboy.

"ROAR!" says the saber-tooth tiger.

Oops! The saber-tooth tiger is still

too hungry. Caveboy and Sister both scream.

AHHHHHHHHH!

They run and run.

When Caveboy and Sister stop, Caveboy catches his breath. He smiles. "Sister," he says, "you are not so boring."

Sister blushes. She opens her mouth to say something. And then . . .

Without warning, Sister lets out a great, big BU-U-U-R-RP!

"Yuck!" Caveboy shouts. He holds his nose. "Sisters *really* do smell like burps!"

Caveboy sees a tear on Sister's cheek. She tries to hide her face.

So Caveboy says, "I love you anyway."

CHAPTER 2
MAMMOTH HUNT

Caveboy and Sister are playing. All of a sudden, they hear a gurgle. It is loud.

Sister stops and looks around. "What was that?" she asks. "A waterfall?"

Caveboy taps his chin. He says, "I do not think it was a waterfall."

Then they hear a rumble. It is very loud.

"What was that?" asks Sister, hiding her head. "A falling tree?"

Caveboy shrugs. He says, "I do not think it was a tree."

Then they hear a growl. It is very, very loud.

"What was that?" asks Sister. "A saber-tooth tiger?"

She lifts up her club to be ready, but she looks a little scared.

Caveboy shakes his head. “I do not think it was a saber-tooth tiger,” he mumbles. He looks down. “I think it was my tummy,” he says.

"Caveboy," Sister asks, "are you hungry?"

Caveboy's tummy growls again. "I think I am," he answers. He scratches his head. "What can I eat?"

"Mama has berries," Sister suggests. "And berries are healthy."

"Berries are boring," mumbles Caveboy. But then his tummy growls again. He needs something to eat that is not

boring. He wants something that is tasty.

Caveboy paces back and forth. He taps his club on the ground to help him think. Suddenly, he has an idea. "I will hunt for food!"

Caveboy sees footprints on the ground. "I will hunt a mammoth!" he shouts.

Sister shakes her head. "Bad idea," she says.

But Caveboy does not listen. He follows the footprints.

Sister follows him.

The footprints go down a hill. They circle around a tree. Then they disappear behind a bush.

"Shh!" Caveboy whispers.

"The mammoth is behind this bush."

Sister shrugs. "I do not think so," she says.

Caveboy gets ready to hunt. He raises his

club. He starts to tiptoe closer. But then, his tummy gurgles. And it is loud.

"No!" groans Caveboy. "Now the mammoth will run away!"

When he peeks behind the bush, there is no mammoth. There are only footprints.

"You cannot eat *that*," Sister says. She points toward home. "You are very hungry. Mama has berries. And berries are healthy *and* juicy."

"Berries are boring," grumbles Caveboy. "I can still hunt for food!"

"Bad idea," says Sister. She rolls her eyes.

Caveboy follows the footprints again. They go across some grass. They turn around a pond. Then they disappear behind a rock.

"Shh!" Caveboy whispers. "The mammoth is behind this rock."

Sister sighs. "No, he is not."

Caveboy gets ready to hunt. He lifts his club high over his head. He starts to take his first step. But then, his tummy rumbles. And it is very loud.

"No!" moans Caveboy. "Now the mammoth will run away!"

When he peeks behind the rock, there are footprints. There

is one more thing, but it is not a mammoth.

Sister says, "You cannot eat *that*."

"Yuck!" shouts Caveboy.

Sister points her club toward home. "You are very, very hungry. Mama has berries. And berries are healthy, juicy, and tasty. And they are not pretend, like this mammoth!"

"Berries are boring," whines Caveboy. "And it is not a pretend mammoth! And I am going to hunt for food!"

Sister smacks her own forehead. "Bad idea," she says.

Caveboy follows the footprints again. They stretch across some mud. They duck under a branch. Then they disappear into a small, dark cave.

"Shh!" Caveboy whispers. "The mammoth is inside this cave."

Sister mumbles, "There is no mammoth inside a cave like this. It is too small for a mammoth. I think hunger is making you loopy."

But Caveboy is not listening. He gets ready to hunt. He hoists his club up. He tiptoes once, then twice, then

three times. He grins. *The mammoth is in here!* he thinks.

But then, his tummy growls. And it is very, very loud.

Before Caveboy can say anything, someone else growls.

"Saber-tooth tiger!" shrieks Sister.

AHHHHHHHHH!

screams Caveboy.

They both run and run.

When Caveboy and Sister are far away, they find a log. They sit down. Sister says, “That was not a mammoth.”

"I know," Caveboy replies.

"And you are still very, very, very hungry," adds Sister.

"I know," Caveboy replies.

"And now I am hungry, too," Sister whines. And her tummy growls.

"Shh!" Caveboy whispers. "Look what I found behind this log." He points. "BERRIES!"

Caveboy and Sister eat berries until their fingers turn purple. They eat until there is juice on their chins.

Then Caveboy says, “I knew I could hunt for food.”

Sister nods. She smiles. Then she lets out a great, big

CHAPTER 3
GO to BED

The sky is dark. The moon is shining. It has been a good day.

Caveboy and Sister played with rocks, trees, and saber-tooth tigers. They hunted for mammoths and berries. When they came back to the

cave, they ate Papa's yummy dinner and played rock-arrow-club with Mama. But now, Caveboy is tired.

Mama sees the yawn. She takes Caveboy's hand and Sister's hand. "I think it is time for you two to go to sleep," she says.

Caveboy nods. But Sister scowls. "I am not sleepy!" she yells.

"It is bedtime," says Mama. "No arguing."

Caveboy nods again. Sister scowls again. But they both go into their room.

Caveboy kisses his pet rock good

night. But Sister is just standing there. So Caveboy says, "We should go to sleep."

Sister crosses her arms. "I am not sleepy!"

Caveboy shrugs. "I am going to bed anyway." He climbs under his blanket. He hugs his club. He closes his eyes.

Then he hears *plop. Plop. Plop*.

Caveboy opens one eye. What is that?

Plop.

It is Sister. Her hands are filled with acorns. She throws one acorn into a puddle. It goes *plop*.

She throws another acorn. *Plop*. *Plop*. *Plop*. *Plop*.

Caveboy throws off his blanket. He yells, "I cannot sleep if you do that!"

But Sister shrugs. And she tosses another acorn. *Plop.*

Caveboy sighs. He rubs his eyes. He is very tired. “I need a plan,” he grumbles. “A plan to make Sister fall asleep.”

Caveboy stands up. He taps his fingers against his club. He is trying to think of a plan.

Suddenly, his eyes light up. *I have an idea!* he thinks.

“Let me tuck you in, Sister,”

Caveboy offers. He holds up Sister's blanket. "I will help you sleep."

"I am not sleepy," Sister whines. But she trudges over to her bed anyway. She gets under her blanket. But she does not lie down.

"Here," says Caveboy. He hands Sister her pet rock. "Try snuggling with this. It will help you sleep."

Sister yawns. She closes her eyes. She lies back and puts her head on the pillow. She snuggles her pet rock.

When Sister is quiet, Caveboy smiles. “That was a good plan,” he whispers to himself. He fixes Sister’s

blanket before he tiptoes back to his bed.

Caveboy quietly climbs under his blanket again. He hugs his club again. He closes his eyes again.

Then he hears *scrape. Scrape. Scraaaaape.*

Caveboy opens both eyes. What is that?

Scrape.

It is Sister. Again. This time, she is scratching her pet rock against the wall. It goes *scrape*.

Scrape. Scrape. Scraaaaape.

"I need another plan," Caveboy mumbles. "A better plan than before."

Caveboy is very, very tired. He drums the ground with his club. He thinks very hard.

Soon, Caveboy has an idea. He throws off his blanket. He goes to Sister. He takes away her pet rock. "Sister," he says, "I have another plan for you to try. I think you should count mammoths. That will help you sleep."

"But what about my pet rock?" Sister asks.

"I will put her back where she belongs," says Caveboy. "Do not worry."

Sister nods.

Caveboy tucks Sister in. She closes her eyes. She whispers, "One mammoth . . . two mammoths . . ." Then she yawns.

Caveboy tiptoes back to his bed. Sister whispers, "Three mammoths . . . four . . . mammoths . . ."

Then Sister stops whispering.

That was a good plan, Caveboy thinks. He climbs under his blanket again. He hugs his club again. He closes his eyes again.

Then he hears *sniffle. Sniffle. Sniffle.*

Caveboy opens both eyes and sits straight up. *What is that?*

Sniffle.

It is Sister. She is crying. “I cannot sleep,” she whines. “I had a bad dream about mammoths. Mammoths are coming to eat me!”

Caveboy rolls his eyes. He grits his teeth. He grumbles, “I need another plan.”

But now, Caveboy is very, very, very tired. His fingers tighten

around his club. He thinks as hard as he can. And then he thinks some more.

Suddenly, Caveboy has an idea. And it is the best idea so far! He throws off his blanket. He gives Sister a hug. He walks her back to her bed.

"Stop counting mammoths," he says. "That was not the right thing to do."

Caveboy fluffs Sister's pillow. He pulls the blanket up to her chin.

He says, "Close your eyes." Then he sings a lullaby.

Rock-a-bye, Sister, here in our cave.
Time to be sleepy, time to behave.
Do not be scared of mammoths a bit,
Your brother is here to make them all split.

When he is done singing, Sister is sleeping. Caveboy smiles. “That was a good plan,” he whispers. “A very, very good plan.”

Caveboy tiptoes back to his bed one more time. He climbs under his blanket one more time. He closes his eyes one more time. He thinks it will be the last time.

Then he hears a loud sound.

He opens one eye. What is that?

ROAR!

Is it a saber-tooth tiger?

ROAR!

No, it is not a saber-tooth tiger. It is Sister. Snoring.

"I cannot sleep if you do that!" Caveboy yells.

Sister's eyes stay closed. She does

not say anything. But then Caveboy hears the sound. Again.

Caveboy cannot believe it. He pulls his blanket over his head.

ROAR!

He tries to cover his ears.

ROAR!

It goes on all night. In the morning, Caveboy rubs his eyes. He yawns and yawns. And then he mutters, “That was not a good plan.”

READ & BLOOM

PLANT THE LOVE OF READING

Agnes and Clarabelle are the best of friends!

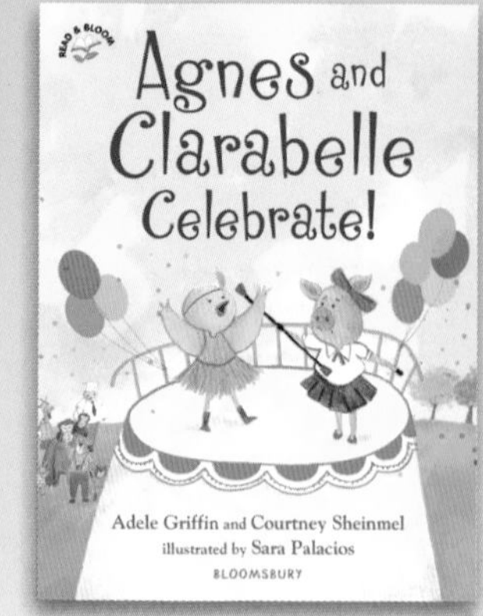

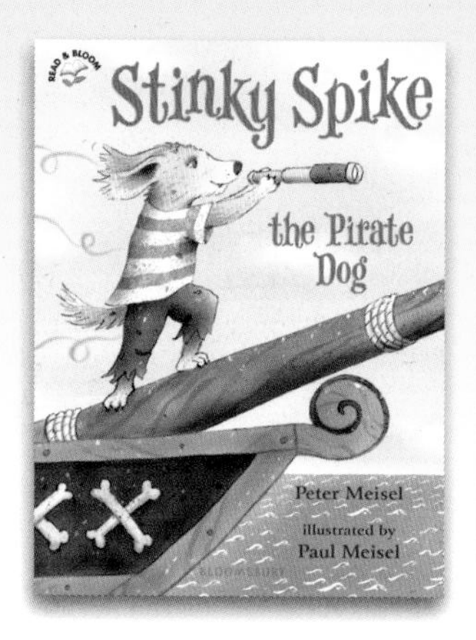

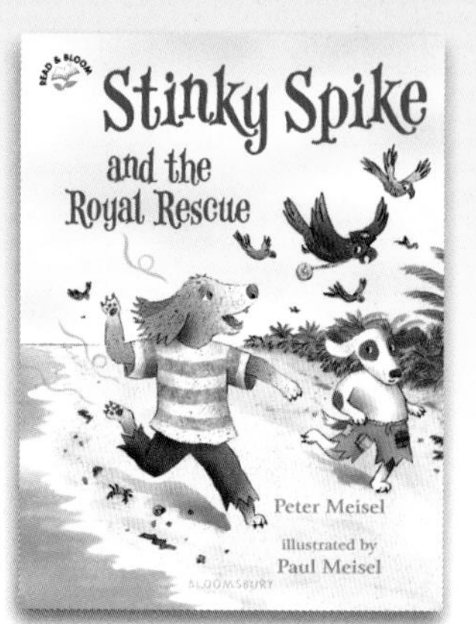

Stinky Spike can sniff his way out of any trouble!

You don't want to miss these great characters! The Read & Bloom line is perfect for newly independent readers. These stories are fully illustrated and bursting with fun!

READ EVERY SERIES!

Caveboy is always ready for an adventure!

Wallace and Grace are owl detectives who solve mysteries!

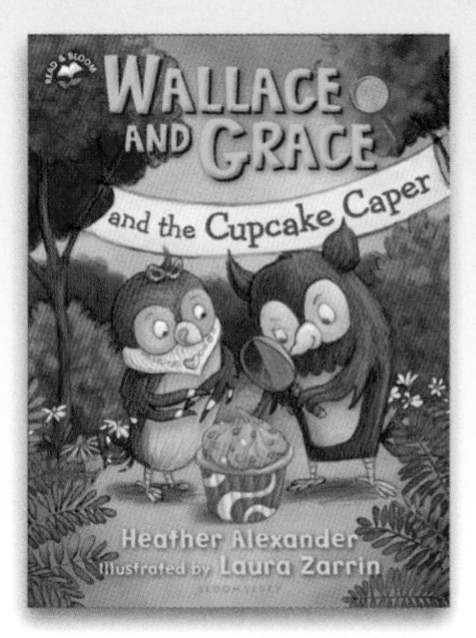

www.bloomsbury.com • Twitter: BloomsburyKids • Facebook: KidsBloomsbury

SUDIPTA BARDHAN-QUALLEN lives in New Jersey with her cavefamily—three cavekids and one cavehusband. She cannot hit baseskulls, hunt saber-tooth tigers, or scare away spiders, but she is very good at reading, traveling, and shopping for shoes. Sudipta is the award-winning author of over forty books for children, including *Duck, Duck, Moose!*, *Tyrannosaurus Wrecks!*, and *Chicks Run Wild*.

sudipta.com

ERIC WIGHT spends a lot of time in his cave making books for children, including the Frankie Pickle and Magic Shop series. When he was a kid, he had a unibrow just like Caveboy. He lives with his wife and herd of children in Chalfont, Pennsylvania.

ericwight.com